Squawk

Squawk

by Megan Gail Coles

Playwrights Canada Press
Toronto

LIBRARY AND ARCHIVES CANADA CATALOGUING IN PUBLICATION
Coles, Megan, author
        Squawk / Megan Gail Coles. -- First edition.

A play.
Issued in print and electronic formats.
ISBN 978-1-77091-818-4 (softcover).--ISBN 978-1-77091-819-1 (PDF).--
ISBN 978-1-77091-820-7 (EPUB).--ISBN 978-1-77091-821-4 (Kindle)

        I. Title.

PS8605.O4479S68 2017   C812'.6   C2017-906254-9
                                                          C2017-906255-7

We acknowledge the financial support of the Canada Council for the Arts, the Ontario Arts Council (OAC), the Ontario Media Development Corporation, and the Government of Canada for our publishing activities.

 Canada Council Conseil des arts
for the Arts du Canada

 ONTARIO ARTS COUNCIL
CONSEIL DES ARTS DE L'ONTARIO
an Ontario government agency
un organisme du gouvernement de l'Ontario

 Canadä

 Ontario
Ontario Media Development
Corporation

Squawk is dedicated to the courageous girl children who have their girlhood jeopardized routinely. And to all the grandmothers who love them well and steady through it. Especially mine.

Playwright's Notes

The *Squawk* commission came upon the heels of a very transformative phase in my mid-adulthood. I was working as a publicist and navigating an unexpected prose career while spending every available moment preoccupied with how I might write an accessible and humorous TYA show about missing and murdered Indigenous girls. To say it was a most challenging assignment is an understatement. I wanted desperately to write a compelling and sophisticated play that provided an opportunity for dialogue across culturally lived experiences. Because the subject matter was very dear to my own heart and very important to our reconciling as a nation. I wanted the youth to fully comprehend that prevailing systemic racism and aggressive misogyny is not acceptable and that we must do something to address this. I want our young people to value and protect each other better in the future.

I write this as predominantly male white supremacy groups escalate mounting racial tension and terror in countries throughout the Western world. They are angry because the historically oppressed have demanded more than the dregs of living for themselves and their loved ones. But we are angry, too. I'm angry. I have quite a lot to be justifiably angry about. Which is to say that this is a play I am most proud of because it is an act of defiance and subversion. I do not consent to social norms that harm vulnerable people. I reject privilege and demand a more inclusive society where all enjoy personal freedom in safety. I feel that art, but theatre especially, has the potential to illuminate the universal right to a dignified life for all and feel strongly that communicating our diverse narratives will move us toward a healthier and happier country.

Thanks to Geordie for insisting, adamantly at times, that I push through the hard stuff and to Emma for her commitment to my work and belief in me. I could never have done it without her. The play is for the special smaller humans in my life. It is for those whom I see daily and for those whom circumstances prevent. I want you all to be kind and well. And to always conduct yourselves in this world with compassion regardless of what is popular, because what is popular is not always right and good. In fact, what is right and good is rarely popular and never easy. But you are smart and strong and I believe in you.

The play is also for my grandmother who was called a terrible name when she was little because of her not nearly white enough skin.

Squawk was developed by Playwrights' Workshop Montréal and first produced by Geordie Productions, Montreal, in September 2015 as a touring play in Quebec high schools and CEGEPs. It featured the following cast and creative team:

Annie: Cheyenne Scott
Isaac: Patrick Abellard
Louis: Gabriel Schultz

Director: Jessica Abdallah
Dramaturg: Emma Tibaldo
Set, Costume, Prop and Production Design: Cathia Pagotto
Sound Design: Troy Slocum
Production Design: George Allister

Isaac and Louis should be cast regardless of ethnicity, and therefore the lines concerning Isaac's ethnicity should be changed to reflect the actor. Annie should be played by an Indigenous woman or girl whenever possible.

Geographic references to things such as Provigo, Montreal and Simons should be changed to reference the predominant grocery store, urban centre and department store nearest the production.

Characters

Annie | Indigenous teenager aging out of care.
Isaac | Teenager Annie meets in a food court.
Louis | Annie's adult care worker.

A flashlight is lit ghost-story style under ANNIE's chin.

ANNIE: I think: here is how I die. One night I walk into the snow until I stop walking. I don't take my coat. I have no mittens. Children wander from houses where I live and no one notices until later. Because parents are passed out on sofas, doors and windows—

ANNIE throws her arms open.

—wide open.

> *Real world. Food court. The neon-coloured lights denote the various restaurant signs, a series of rectangular boxes stacked atop one another. There are three restaurants, nine boxes total. Perhaps red, yellow and green: stop, slow, go. ISAAC happens upon ANNIE playing her game.*
>
> *ISAAC looks at her phone.*

ISAAC: My little sister plays that.

She pulls away.

ANNIE: Yay for her.

ISAAC: She's seven.

ANNIE: And next year she'll be eight. That's how counting works.

ISAAC: How old are you?

ANNIE: Umm, do I know you?

ISAAC: No.

ANNIE makes a move-along motion with her head.

There are way better games you can play.

ANNIE: I like this one.

ISAAC: You just don't know.

ANNIE: Right. Next you'll tell me what music I should listen to.

ISAAC: Why would I do that?

ANNIE: Because that's what boys do.

ISAAC: Do we?

ANNIE: Yeah huh. Boys think they know everything because they're boys.

ISAAC: You just don't know about the different games.

ANNIE: You don't know what I know.

ISAAC: There's *DayZ*. Or *Dead Rising*. *Resident Evil*.

ANNIE: I don't want to play those games.

ISAAC: Or *GTA*.

ANNIE: Definitely not interested in games like that.

ISAAC: It's like the best game of all time.

ANNIE: Oh really?

ISAAC: Yeah.

ANNIE: And you think I'd like it?

ISAAC: Everyone does.

ANNIE: You think I would enjoy playing that game?

ISAAC: You'd love it.

ANNIE: I'd love it?

ISAAC: Definitely.

ANNIE: You're sure?

ISAAC: Positive.

ANNIE: A game where you make women do sex stuff for money? I'd love that game?

ISAAC: Wait. What?

ANNIE: Make poor women do sex stuff because they're hungry or on drugs or cold. Is that the game you think I'd love?

ISAAC: I didn't say that.

ANNIE: Should I play a game where women get killed so you can steal from them? Is that the game you want me to play after talking to me for two minutes? You want me to play your disgusting murder game?

Beat.

ISAAC: It's a car-racing game.

ANNIE: It's not.

ISAAC: The part you're talking about isn't even a big deal in the game.

ANNIE: That makes it worse.

ISAAC: It's the smallest move you can make really.

ANNIE: Exactly.

ISAAC: They're not even important.

ANNIE: They're not even important.

ISAAC: They're just in the background.

ANNIE: See. It doesn't even matter to you.

ISAAC: What doesn't even matter?

ANNIE: All the dead girls.

ISAAC: Dead girls?

ANNIE: In the games you play!

ISAAC: It's pretend.

ANNIE: Who wants to pretend that?

ISAAC: Millions of people.

ANNIE: Why?

ISAAC: It's exciting.

ANNIE: It's awful.

ISAAC: Make believe.

ANNIE: Common place.

ISAAC: Fantasy stuff.

ANNIE: But it's not!

ISAAC: What?

ANNIE: It's not fantasy! The scary things in your games happen.

ISAAC: What?

ANNIE: Forget it. You wouldn't understand.

ISAAC: Why not?

ANNIE: 'Cause you're from here.

ISAAC: Yeah.

ANNIE: 'Cause you're a boy.

ISAAC: So.

ANNIE: 'Cause you're not Indigenous.

ISAAC: Pfft. That's kind of like totally racist.

ANNIE: It's kind of like totally true.

   Beat.

ISAAC: So . . . what are you then?

ANNIE: What am I?

ISAAC: What kind of Native? I know there are different kinds and stuff.

ANNIE: Different kinds and stuff?

ISAAC: It's hard to tell. Your face is a kind of puzzle.

ANNIE: Is my face confusing for you?

ISAAC: Why'd you pierce your nose?

ANNIE: Why'd you wear a blue shirt?

ISAAC: The colour of my shirt is not the same as the hole in your face.

ANNIE: Don't catastrophize.

ISAAC: Why though?

ANNIE: I don't know. Wanted to be different.

ISAAC: Something tells me you're plenty different out of the gate.

ANNIE: Look different. Not like me. Like someone else.

ISAAC: Who?

ANNIE: No one special.

   Beat.

You've never wanted to be someone . . . better?

ISAAC: Better you has a hoop in her nose?

ANNIE: She might. Besides, all the women in my family try to look different. My grandmother has been dying her hair for so long she can't remember what colour her hair was. I had to tell her it wasn't brown. I had to show her a picture of her black hair.

ISAAC: Weird.

ANNIE: My grandmother is all kinds of weird. She wants us to go live in the woods. She wants us to walk millions of miles across the tundra until we find what we lost.

ISAAC: What did you lose?

ANNIE: I don't know. But she thinks the only way to get to it is on foot.

Beat.

ISAAC: I thought you were Asian first, Japanese or something.

ANNIE: Not Japanese. Never been to Japan.

ISAAC: You could almost pass for a white girl.

ANNIE: Who said anything about passing for a white girl?

ISAAC: I didn't mean anything by it.

ANNIE: Then why say it?

ISAAC: Because I was thinking it.

ANNIE: You shouldn't say everything you think.

ISAAC: I was also thinking you kind of look like a cat but I didn't say that.

ANNIE: You just did.

ISAAC: What?

ANNIE: Said I look like a cat. But I'm not a cat, am I?

ISAAC: No, not a cat.

ANNIE: Girl human.

ISAAC: Girl human.

ANNIE: Yeah, and you're a parrot.

ISAAC: What?

ANNIE: What?

ISAAC: What?

ANNIE: What!

Beat.

ISAAC: I'm Isaac.

ANNIE: Sure.

ISAAC: And you are?

ANNIE: Occupied.

ISAAC: Occupied? That's an odd name.

ANNIE: It's not my name.

ISAAC: Nice to meet you, Occupied.

ANNIE: My name is not Occupied.

ISAAC: Like a toilet.

ANNIE: Not like a toilet.

ISAAC: On an airplane.

ANNIE: Or an airplane.

ISAAC: Like a tiny bathroom.

ANNIE: I'm not talking to you anymore.

ISAAC: With a little nameplate you can slide.

ANNIE: I'm not listening to you.

ISAAC: Unoccupied.

ANNIE: Basically, you're talking to yourself.

ISAAC: Occupied!

ANNIE: I hear nothing—

ISAAC: That's you.

ANNIE: —no words at all.

ISAAC: You're Occupied.

ANNIE: It's Annie.

ISAAC: Annie?

ANNIE: My name. It's Annie Runningbird.

ISAAC: Annie Runningbird. Great name.

> *LOUIS returns carrying a basket of fries. He does not give them to ANNIE.*

LOUIS: There you are.

ANNIE: Here I am.

LOUIS: I couldn't find you.

ANNIE: You found me.

LOUIS: I had to look.

ANNIE: How inconvenient for you.

LOUIS: What did I say about your attitude?

ANNIE: I don't know. A lot?

LOUIS: And who's this? Stranger, is it?

ISAAC: I'm Isaac.

LOUIS: Nice to meet you, Isaac. I'm Louis.

ANNIE: He's my babysitter.

LOUIS: I'm her care worker.

ANNIE: I'm in-care. Woot woot.

ISAAC: What's in-care?

LOUIS: She doesn't live with her family.

ANNIE: Ward of the state. Louis's a spy for the government of Canada, don't ya know?

LOUIS: I actually work for a private-care company.

ANNIE: A valid driver's licence and a clear driving abstract make him uniquely qualified to manage my emotional problems.

LOUIS: Annie. That's . . . not even true. You need post-secondary. I have a Classics degree.

ISAAC: What's it like?

LOUIS: A B.A.? Kind of useless.

ISAAC: No, ward of the state. Where do you live?

ANNIE: A hotel. Or a motel. I don't know the difference really. An apartment. It has a tiny oven and a toaster so it's different from a normal kind of room.

LOUIS: It's a temporary solution to an ongoing capacity issue.

ISAAC: Sounds great.

ANNIE: It's not great. Great is not the right word.

ISAAC: What's the right word?

ANNIE: There is no right word.

LOUIS: It's adequate and better than the alternative.

ISAAC: Alternative?

ANNIE: There's this building everyone calls the "centre" though I don't what it's the centre of. Hell, maybe.

LOUIS: Language.

ANNIE: I thought it was the worst because all the kids were shitty to each other—

LOUIS: Watch your mouth.

ANNIE: —but there are worse places.

ISAAC: Really?

ANNIE: Yeah. In this other place there was a cook who didn't believe in cheese. Said she had no faith in dairy like food was religion.

LOUIS: Budgetary challenges are a factor.

ANNIE: Curds were like a weapon for evil.

LOUIS: Cheese is expensive.

ANNIE: Poutine was like French-Canadian witchcraft.

LOUIS: And poutine makes people fat.

ANNIE: This cook suggested I meditate about my "situation" and drink smoothies. She was nice enough but right crunchy.

ISAAC: What's your situation?

ANNIE: This is my situation. He's my situation.

LOUIS: Your lack of gratitude is frightening.

ANNIE: Listening to Louis is like choking on a Life Saver.

LOUIS: Do you know why you're striking out, Annie? Right now?

ISAAC: Maybe, I should go—

LOUIS: Maybe you should.

ANNIE: Oh, hell.

LOUIS: Language.

ANNIE: Hell is not language, Louis! It's place.

ISAAC: Right, place. I have to be at a place. Not this place. A different place. Over there somewhere. That place.

ANNIE: You can stay.

LOUIS: It was nice to meet you, Isaac.

ANNIE: You don't have to go because he says so.

ISAAC: Umm . . . I should probably—

ANNIE: He's not the boss of you.

LOUIS: Annie!

ANNIE: What?

LOUIS: Manners.

ANNIE: You're not. You're not even the boss of me. I'm the boss of me. Grandmother said.

LOUIS: Knock off the squawking, Annie!

ISAAC: What time of day is it anyway? Must be dark outside. You can't tell in the mall. Mom probably needs help with her zipper or her purse or her phone. Or something. So, I have to go. So, so, bye.

ISAAC leaves. ANNIE reaches for the fries. LOUIS pulls them back.

LOUIS: Who was that?

ANNIE: I don't know.

LOUIS: You were talking to him.

ANNIE: He was talking to me.

LOUIS: You just can't talk to strangers. Who knows what he wants from you?

ANNIE: I do.

LOUIS: What does he want?

ANNIE: He wants me to play his games.

LOUIS: Games? What kind of games? Are you wearing all your clothes in these games? Are they kissing games?

ANNIE: What? I don't know. Yes. No. Yuck. You're so gross.

LOUIS: Did he ask you to get in his car?

ANNIE: People my age don't have cars.

LOUIS: You can't trust people.

ANNIE: I know you can't trust people.

LOUIS: Wow. You really are rude today. *(whispers)* Are you on your period?

ANNIE: What? No!

LOUIS: Maybe your blood sugar is low. When did you eat last?

ANNIE: I don't remember.

She reaches for the fries again.

LOUIS: If you don't remember, then you need to eat.

ANNIE: I'm fricken trying to.

LOUIS: Language.

ANNIE: I didn't say it.

LOUIS: No, but you were thinking it on the inside. And that is like saying it. Will evolve into saying it. Cursing is a weak form of communication.

ANNIE: Sorry.

LOUIS: Don't just say you're sorry. Learn from your mistakes, Annie, and the mistakes of others.

ANNIE: Can I please have my fries now? I'm so hungry. It's making me right irritable.

LOUIS: You must be in a state of ever-constant starvation if that's the case.

ANNIE: Don't joke.

LOUIS: Maybe you have a tapeworm.

ANNIE: Not funny.

She grabs for the fries again.

LOUIS: You'll end up with diabetes like your grandmother.

ANNIE: Whatever.

LOUIS: She'll probably lose a foot.

ANNIE: That doesn't happen anymore.

LOUIS: It does. Loss of lower limbs is common in people like you.

ANNIE: People like me?

LOUIS: Indigenous people. Search it up.

ANNIE: Well that's not fair. Someone should do something about it—sue the government or something.

LOUIS: Your crowd tried that already, didn't work. Besides, it's not Canada's fault if you don't take care. Drink. Smoke. Eat dirty food.

LOUIS throws the fries down in front of her.

ANNIE: But how will she walk?

LOUIS: She won't.

ANNIE: But how will she get places?

LOUIS: Wheelchair?

ANNIE: In the snow?

LOUIS: Dog team.

ANNIE: Dog team? She's eighty.

Beat.

LOUIS: Eat your dinner before it gets cold.

He pushes the basket of fries toward her. ANNIE stares at the fries.

Or don't, but that's what you're getting. It's what you wanted.

ANNIE starts to eat the fries.

So what kind of games did that boy want to play? Board games, hockey games—

ANNIE: No, games.

LOUIS: Video games?

ANNIE: Only old people say video games.

LOUIS: I'm not old. I play games. I'm a gamer.

ANNIE: Sure you are.

LOUIS: I have a whole life outside of buying you junk food, you know? I have interests. Goals. You don't even know what I'm into.

ANNIE: Don't even want to know.

LOUIS: Don't be a brat, Annie.

Beat.

ANNIE: Were you talking to Sharon?

LOUIS: I can't believe you call your social worker by her first name.

ANNIE: I've known her since I was eleven.

LOUIS: Still.

ANNIE: What'd she say?

LOUIS: Lots. Sharon always has lots to say. Talkative: that Sharon.

ANNIE: And?

Beat.

LOUIS: Your cousin had her baby.

ANNIE: Really? Which one?

LOUIS: The one with the bad arm.

ANNIE: Diane.

LOUIS: Yeah. The one with the bad arm.

ANNIE: What did she have?

LOUIS: A boy.

ANNIE: A boy!

LOUIS: And then a girl.

ANNIE: And then a girl?

LOUIS: Twins.

ANNIE: Two little babies!

LOUIS: That's what happens when you don't take care.

ANNIE: How adorifying.

LOUIS: Adorifying?

ANNIE: When things are so adorable that it's horrifying.

LOUIS: I've never heard that before. You make that up?

ANNIE: A girl at the motel said it.

LOUIS: Clever.

ANNIE: She's right clever. She might be the smartest girl in the world.

LOUIS: Hyperbole, Annie.

ANNIE: Hyperbole?

LOUIS: Exaggerating. Girls your age, I've noticed, like to exaggerate.

ANNIE: Well, she's the smartest girl I've ever met.

LOUIS: I guess I can accept that given the girls you know. Which girl is this?

ANNIE: Umm . . . just a girl.

LOUIS: Which one?

ANNIE: One of the housekeepers.

LOUIS: Which housekeeper?

ANNIE: You probably don't know her.

LOUIS: I know all the housekeepers.

ANNIE: Can't remember her name.

LOUIS: You can't remember the name of the smartest girl you've ever met?

ANNIE: Bad memory.

LOUIS: I don't believe you.

ANNIE: No one ever believes me.

LOUIS: Who was it?

ANNIE: It might have been Therese.

LOUIS: Therese? She doesn't know what's good for her. Don't listen to anything she says. She's a liar.

ANNIE: She didn't tell me any lies.

LOUIS: Did she say anything about me?

ANNIE: She didn't mention your name.

LOUIS: Oh really, not once?

ANNIE: Never said your name, not once. Honest.

LOUIS: Good. She's not a good girl, Therese. She makes up stories. You can't trust girls who make up stories.

ANNIE: Gotcha. Don't trust girl storytellers.

LOUIS: I'm serious. Don't be friendly with her.

ANNIE: I said fine. There's no point anyway.

LOUIS: Why's that?

ANNIE: Because I'm going home on my birthday.

LOUIS: Going home?

ANNIE: The moment I age out.

LOUIS: Why? There's nothing for you up there.

ANNIE: Grandmother's there.

LOUIS: Don't be foolish. Nothing but poverty and pain where you're from.

ANNIE: There's more than poverty and pain. That's ridiculous.

LOUIS: Snow and starving polar bears.

ANNIE: And whose fault is that?

LOUIS: Beats me. I'm no scientist.

ANNIE: Understatement of the year.

LOUIS: Listen, the city is where everything happens.

ANNIE: What is everything, exactly?

LOUIS: You know. New beginnings. Fresh starts.

ANNIE: Fresh? There's nothing fresh about this place. It stinks here. A person can barely breathe. There's no air.

LOUIS: There's air.

ANNIE: Not air that hasn't already been hauled in and blown out by millions of strangers. Who wants second-hand air? All carbon monoxide and exhaust fumes and cigarette smoke and sweat and perfume and farts. Yuck.

LOUIS: You're kind of pretty when you're worked up.

ANNIE: Don't say that.

LOUIS: It's true. You should be told how pretty you are.

ANNIE: Stop.

LOUIS: You're like a tiny Runningbird, you know.

> *LOUIS touches her wrist. We enter ANNIE's game world. The three restaurants—nine boxes total—red, yellow and green illuminate the scene. A box reads "play game." LOUIS is now in a car.*

My skills have been tested on and off the battlefield.

ANNIE: I refuse to play with you.

LOUIS: You can't resist me; my pheromones are hunters.

ANNIE: That's preposterous.

LOUIS: If you do start to grow restless, I will seize you.

ANNIE: Gross.

LOUIS: I have resources that outnumber your resources.

ANNIE: I don't want your money.

LOUIS: There are different ways to earn points with me.

ANNIE: I don't need your points.

LOUIS: Points are necessary to track your progress through the game.

ANNIE: You're a really sad man.

LOUIS: I'm a great soldier. No more. No less.

ANNIE: No more is right.

LOUIS: I will continue to pursue my objective in order to survive.

ANNIE: That has nothing to do with me.

LOUIS: But it does. You're my new mission. I need your power.

ANNIE: Get your own power.

LOUIS: I need my power and your power. I need everything. And you need me.

ANNIE: What for?

LOUIS: To protect you from the opposition. Princesses need protecting or they fall from tall buildings into fast-moving rivers. They get locked in castles when left unprotected.

ANNIE: What kind of castle?

LOUIS: There are different kinds. But they are all cold, dark places you need saving from.

ANNIE: Where are they?

LOUIS: On paths. Alleys. Walking trails. Inside houses. Hotels. Motels. Rooms. Behind schools. Parks. Playgrounds. Bus stops. Grocery stores. Clubs. Bars. Campgrounds. Cabins.

ANNIE: I just won't go to those places. I'll stay away from all those places.

LOUIS: You can't stay away from everywhere.

ANNIE: Things don't happen everywhere.

LOUIS: Everywhere girls are: things happen.

Beat.

You need me. I can keep you safe.

ANNIE: I don't want your help.

LOUIS: Resistance is futile.

ANNIE: I will resist. All the times. Forever.

LOUIS: You're a stubborn princess. But even stubborn princesses deserve pity.

LOUIS reveals a baggy.

These are for you.

ANNIE: No thanks. I'm good.

LOUIS: To rescue you.

ANNIE: I'll rescue myself.

LOUIS: Then they're a reward for your hard work at rescuing yourself.

ANNIE: You can't ingest rewards.

LOUIS: Of course you can. Rewards are the easiest thing to swallow.

ANNIE: I'm allergic to your fake rewards. They make me sick.

LOUIS: Take them. Don't take them. Your choice.

ANNIE: Life is full of choices.

LOUIS: The only choice is where you are when your game ends.

A flashlight illuminates from under a door.

ANNIE: I think: no, here is how I die. One night I swallow all the house-fire smoke seeping under my bared bedroom door. There is a chair against it and uncle is getting angry downstairs while I sleep and no one knows until later. Because adults are drinking in the abandoned school where teachers smacked their faces or their bottoms. Or worse.

Real world. Food court. ANNIE is playing her game. ISAAC arrives with fries, puts them in front of her.

ISAAC: I bought you a basket of fries.

ANNIE: I didn't ask you for fries.

ISAAC: They're sweet potato.

LOUIS approaches.

ANNIE: Shit. He's coming! Hide!

ANNIE pulls ISAAC down under the table. He reaches up and gets the fries. They eat them under the table.

LOUIS: Why are we under the table?

She puts a forefinger to her lips. They are quiet. ISAAC reaches forward and ties her shoe.

ANNIE: Stop that.

ISAAC: Stop what?

ANNIE: What you're doing?

She swipes his hand away from her strings.

ISAAC: You don't like having your laces tied?

ANNIE: I can do it myself.

ISAAC: I'm just trying to be nice.

ANNIE: Try something else.

ISAAC: Like what?

ANNIE: Ask me a question.

ISAAC: What kind of question?

ANNIE: You have to figure that out on your own.

ISAAC: Talking was your idea.

ANNIE: Yes, but I can't talk for you. That's not how a conversation works.

ISAAC: I know how conversation works.

ANNIE: Prove it. Start one.

ISAAC: I can't now; you made it too much pressure.

ANNIE: Don't blame me.

ISAAC: You built it up too much.

ANNIE: You're still doing it.

ISAAC: I didn't want to tie your dumb shoe anyway.

ANNIE: Now you feel stupid so you're being mean.

ISAAC: I do not—am not.

ANNIE: You said my shoe was dumb because I didn't want you to tie my laces.

ISAAC: But I wanted to—

ANNIE: What you want is not more important than what I want.

ISAAC: You want to do everything all by yourself.

ANNIE: You shouldn't rely on people. It's a bad habit.

ISAAC: Everyone relies on someone.

ANNIE: Not me. I rely on just myself.

ISAAC: Well, you don't seem very reliable.

ANNIE: I'm fine. I'll be fine.

ANNIE gets up and out from under the table. ISAAC hops up too.

ISAAC: What are you doing Saturday?

ANNIE: How should I know? It's only Tuesday.

ISAAC: I know, I know. I just— I'm afraid you'll make plans.

ANNIE: What kind of plans?

ISAAC: Other plans . . . with other people.

ANNIE: Oh?

ISAAC: So, do you want to hang out or something? Like, eat food? Or something?

ANNIE: We're eating food now.

ISAAC: More food. Different food. I believe strongly in cheese.

ANNIE: Really?

ISAAC: I'm a cheese believer.

ANNIE: Pfft. Cheese believer.

ISAAC: I worship at the wheel of cheddar.

ANNIE: You're so weird.

ISAAC: Weird in the best way.

ANNIE: Maybe.

ISAAC: So, do you want to go eat cheese with me on Saturday? They put it on everything now. Burgers, pizza, it comes in stick form—

ANNIE: Like a date?

ISAAC: Like a date.

ANNIE: I don't date *[ISAAC's race]* guys.

ISAAC: Now, that is definitely racist.

ANNIE: I don't date white guys or brown guys or any guys of any colour, either. I mean I don't date.

ISAAC: No dating?

ANNIE: Undatable.

ISAAC: That's not a thing.

ANNIE: It is a thing. Me. I'm it.

ISAAC: Why?

ANNIE: Lost my privs.

ISAAC: Your what?

ANNIE: Privileges.

ISAAC: You lost your privileges?

ANNIE: Um-hmm. Yup. I didn't have many to lose.

ISAAC: How did you lose them?

ANNIE: I moved some things, broke some things. I'm a girl. I was born.

ISAAC: That's too bad. Not that you're a girl. Or being born. I mean the lost privileges part, I mean.

ANNIE: No big deal.

ISAAC: Will you get them back?

ANNIE: I'm going to try. I mean, I'm trying. Always trying. But whatever. It doesn't matter, I don't care. Besides, that's how my cousin ended up with twins.

ISAAC: Twins?

ANNIE: You know? Two babies.

ISAAC: From eating a cheeseburger?

ANNIE: Starts with a cheeseburger, then a pizza, then a stick. Before you know it, bam! Halves on a baby. Or two, in my cousin's case.

ISAAC: Double the fun.

ANNIE: No. Double the crying, double the diapers, double the garbage, double the dogs tearing open the garbage—

ISAAC: Why do the dogs tear open the garbage?

ANNIE: Because they're hungry. Duh.

ISAAC: But why are they hungry?

ANNIE: Because no one feeds them. God.

ISAAC: Why not?

ANNIE: Because they don't belong to anyone, okay?

ISAAC: They're wild? You have wild dogs?

ANNIE: Lots of places do.

ISAAC: We don't.

ANNIE: That's because you're first. And I'm not.

ISAAC: Are you second?

ANNIE: Not even.

ISAAC: Third?

ANNIE: I don't get a number. Not even in line. On no radar.

ISAAC: You're on my radar.

ANNIE: Ugh. Gag me. You're so honest.

ISAAC: Mom says honesty is the best policy.

ANNIE: Barf.

ISAAC: I'm sure your cousin will be a great mom.

ANNIE: I'm not. I don't know how she'll be able to take care of one baby. Let alone two. She has a bad arm.

ISAAC: Her husband will help.

ANNIE: What husband?

ISAAC: Then the dad.

ANNIE: Yeah, right. He's why she has a bad arm.

ISAAC: What happened?

ANNIE: They were at a party. There were drinks. Stairs. I don't know. Things happen.

ISAAC: Yeah, of course, things happen.

Beat.

What things happen?

ANNIE: Bad things. Bad things happen to girls and then people say they made those things happen by being in the place where they could. But, but sometimes, Isaac, it's not your fault you're in that place. Sometimes your mom goes away and your grandma gets sick and the government puts you right in the kind of place where these things happen, right with the kind of person who would do them, has done them.

ISAAC: Did a bad thing happen to you, Annie?

ANNIE: Not me.

ISAAC: Who?

ANNIE: I can't tell you. It's not my secret.

ISAAC: Who's secret is it?

ANNIE: Sheesh. You're like a seal pup.

ISAAC: You're changing the subject.

ANNIE: And you're right stunned.

ISAAC: You're still doing it.

ANNIE: So let me.

ISAAC: Fine. Do you eat seal pups?

ANNIE: No! Baby animals. Yuck.

ISAAC: Do you eat seals?

ANNIE: Sure. Adult animals. Yum.

ISAAC: That's disgusting.

ANNIE: Do you eat chicken?

ISAAC: Everyone eats chicken.

ANNIE: Same thing. Worse.

ISAAC: No.

ANNIE: Your belt is made of cow.

ISAAC: That's different.

ANNIE: Yeah, it is. Seals are free.

ISAAC: Until you eat them.

ANNIE: And they are delicious.

ISAAC: Really?

ANNIE: Yeah. They're super food.

ISAAC: Like goji berries.

ANNIE: I don't know what that is.

ISAAC: You don't know what a goji berry is?

ANNIE: No. Those don't grow where I'm from.

ISAAC: You don't have goji berries?

ANNIE: No.

LOUIS: Not even at Provigo?

ANNIE: What's Provigo?

ISAAC: Pfft. You must be from the moon.

ANNIE: No, Isaac, I'm not from the moon; I'm from the North. Food is expensive. And sometimes there's no food to buy. So no, we don't get your fancy berry. I never tasted a peach until I was nine. Soft fruit is for southerners and city people. And no, I don't like your angry games and I don't want to hear about your awesome mom or go on some silly date, and I don't like your stupid orange french fries. French fries are supposed to be yellow—yellow, Isaac! Okay? Is that okay with you?

ISAAC: Woah. Sorry. I'm sorry. I didn't mean to—don't be upset please. I, I don't know how to be around you.

ANNIE: And that's my fault?

ISAAC: I didn't say that. It's just . . . I'm kind of obsessed with you in a non-creepy way.

ANNIE: Oh yeah?

ISAAC: Yeah. I sometimes have imaginary conversations with you.

ANNIE: That's actually kind of creepy.

ISAAC: No, I mean, I think of things I want to tell you.

ANNIE: We just met a couple weeks ago. We're practically strangers.

ISAAC: I know that. But I think you're . . . okay.

ANNIE: Okay? Gee, thanks.

ISAAC: No, like, I think you're better than okay. I think you're great.

ANNIE: Oh?

ISAAC: I might like you.

ANNIE: Might?

ISAAC: Not might. For sure for sure.

ANNIE: Yeah, okay, I like you fine enough.

ISAAC: No, I think I might maybe like-like you. Like I would pause my game when you were talking like you.

ANNIE: Right.

ISAAC: Do you like me like that, a little?

ANNIE: I don't know.

ISAAC: At all?

ANNIE: I like you more than a pretzel or like a sandwich or something. You're better than a pickle.

ISAAC: Excellent! So, we should do something together, if you want, but if you don't then, yuck, me neither.

ANNIE: We could. But only if you want, if you're super sure, 'cause if you're not sure, then I didn't say yes. You imagined it. You've gone and lost your mind.

ISAAC: Not imagining it. Mind not lost. Found.

ANNIE: Okay.

ISAAC touches ANNIE's face as LOUIS returns. He finds them.

LOUIS: Annie, what are you doing?

ANNIE: Eating fries.

She shoves a fry in ISAAC's mouth. He gags a little.

LOUIS: You're going to end up just like your mom if you're not careful, missy.

ANNIE: What if I do, so what?

LOUIS: So what? So where is she?

ANNIE: Leave me alone, Louis.

LOUIS: Tell your new friend where your mom is.

ANNIE: I can't. You know I can't.

LOUIS: Tell him why you can't.

ISAAC: You can tell me, Annie.

ANNIE: But I can't.

ISAAC: You can—

ANNIE shoves more fries in his mouth.

Through chewing:

—you can tell me anything.

ANNIE: You don't understand.

LOUIS: Make him understand.

ANNIE: No. No, I can't.

ISAAC: Annie—

More fries in.

ANNIE: It's no use, Isaac. There's no point.

ISAAC: You can tell me. Promise.

ANNIE: But I can't, Isaac!

More fries.

I can't tell you where my mom is because I don't know where she is!

Beat. ISAAC is chewing and swallowing hard.

She's lost. Kind of.

LOUIS: You don't kind of lose someone.

ANNIE: We kind of lose people all the time.

ISAAC: How?

ANNIE: She moved here. She said there was nothing for her in the community so she went looking for something.

LOUIS: Your mom said that there was nothing for her at home. She said that even though you were there. You were her daughter and you were nothing.

ISAAC: I'm sure she didn't mean you, Annie.

ANNIE: No. No. That's not what she meant. She called me. At first there were phone calls every week. And then sometimes. And then not at all. We called the police. We said she was missing. We asked them to look for her. But they didn't. So we did. Grandmother and I, we came to Montreal.

ISAAC: How old were you?

ANNIE: Little.

LOUIS: You were four. It says in your file your mother left when you were four years old.

ANNIE: I don't remember very much about that time.

LOUIS: Probably a good thing.

ANNIE: Grandmother thinks so. She doesn't want me to have bad memories. With Grandmother it's always so much love. She took me everywhere when I was small, never out of sight; she taught me everything. Berry-picking in August, the house smelling of bake-apple jam; skinning rabbits over the laundry tub, their little fur coats unzipped with one stroke of her fish fillet knife, slid off in a single tug. Look, Annie, Grammy has a bunny. Look at Grammy's bunny. Fine fur trim for my hoods. Nanny's little princess. White people are impressed peeling apples: Grandmother pelted seals on the white linoleum floor and you would never know. Spotless. She's like magic.

ISAAC: Why don't you live with her? She sounds great.

ANNIE: She is but she wants to live in a tent. She wants me to snare small game, to be on the land, hunting and fishing. She wants to walk everywhere. And now she can't even do that. She's not well.

LOUIS: Because she didn't take care. She didn't look out.

ANNIE: She talks about following the caribou herd. She dreams about us eating seal meat every day. Everything you need is handy to you, that's what she says. Everything you need. Right there on the pack ice.

ISAAC: I thought you liked seal meat.

ANNIE: I do. But I also like onion rings. And the Internet. And Taylor Swift. And I don't want to hide away in the woods. Or be sad. Or sleep in parks.

ISAAC: Why would you have to sleep in the park?

ANNIE: Because I'm aging out next week.

ISAAC: I don't know what that means.

LOUIS: She's too old for foster care.

ISAAC: Where will you go?

ANNIE: Out in the world.

ISAAC: Where though?

ANNIE: I don't know. Somewhere.

ISAAC: How will I find you?

LOUIS: You won't.

ANNIE: I'll be missing.

ISAAC: Girls just don't go missing, Annie.

ANNIE: Girls like me go missing. One day they are mowing grass or going ice-skating. Then gone. One day they are hanging Christmas lights or enrolled in nursing school. Then gone. Hundreds of them. Thousands.

ISAAC: I'll come find you. I'll look for you.

ANNIE: Don't say that.

ISAAC: Why?

ANNIE: Because then I'll expect you to and you won't and then I'll be disappointed when you don't find me. It will make me more lost. More alone.

ISAAC: No, really, I'll look. I promise. I won't let you get lost.

LOUIS: You won't look; you wouldn't even know how to look.

ANNIE: He's right. No one knows how to look. Not even the adults. Not even Grandmother. When we got to Montreal, we were so . . . lonesome. We had posters. We walked around. Got lost. People didn't want to talk to us. Or couldn't. We felt like no one cared she was missing.

ISAAC: I care.

LOUIS: You don't even know her.

ISAAC: I know enough. Really. I want to help you.

ISAAC gives ANNIE the last fry.

ANNIE: I look for her in the faces of women on the street. I stare at strangers and wonder if they are my mother. I worry I wouldn't even recognize her so I look for myself. I search faces for parts of me that I think are missing with her. Eyes. Smile. Cheekbones. I don't see her anywhere. Or worse, I saw her and I didn't know. One time, I thought I found her under a pile of newspapers. But it was someone else's mother.

Beat.

ISAAC: You could come live with me.

ANNIE: What?

ISAAC: You could live at my house.

ANNIE: You don't have a house.

ISAAC: I can ask my mom.

LOUIS: She will never say yes.

ISAAC: She will.

ANNIE: Really?

LOUIS: She will never let some Native girl move in to her house, Annie. That's what you are to her. Some Native girl.

ISAAC: I'll ask her. My older sister's in university. You can sleep in her room.

LOUIS: Do you really think his sister wants you sleeping in her bed? You aren't Goldilocks. This is not a fairy-tale story.

ISAAC: She has a purple canopy bed and a record player!

ANNIE: A purple canopy bed!

ISAAC: Mom's just at Simons. I'll go get her. You'll see. I'll be right back. I'll be right back.

ISAAC leaves.

LOUIS: He's never coming back.

ANNIE: He might.

LOUIS: He won't.

Beat. Time passes.

ANNIE: He's not coming back.

LOUIS: No. He isn't.

LOUIS reaches across the table and takes ANNIE's hands in his hands. We enter ANNIE's game world. A box reads "resume game." The scoreboard runs to reflect the scene.

The only reason I have taken this mission is to get closer to my objective.

ANNIE's scoreboard runs danger points.

No matter what happens, I will reach my target.

ANNIE: Target? Who's the target? What's the target?

LOUIS: Revealing my manoeuvres will put my success in jeopardy.

ANNIE: I don't like secrets anymore.

LOUIS: Classified intel must remain classified until an opportunity to strike is imminent.

ANNIE: You shouldn't do things you need to hide.

ANNIE's scoreboard moves ahead one hundred safety points, back to zero.

LOUIS: It's not my style to lurk in the shadows but the world has forced me underground.

ANNIE: I like it above ground. I am an above ground kind of girl.

ANNIE's scoreboard moves ahead healthy points plus bonus yay points.

LOUIS: That's what you've been led to believe by the opposition.

ANNIE: Nope. Nope, that's what I know. Self-taught.

LOUIS: My years of recon have taught me to suspect any other way.

ANNIE: My way is a good way because it's mine.

LOUIS: I was on a path like you once, before I got correct.

ANNIE: The path I'm on is just fine, thanks. I will navigate it myself.

LOUIS: Do you have a partner to help steer?

ANNIE: Steer what? I'm a teenager.

LOUIS: Is there a person who cares for your sense of direction?

ANNIE: No . . . not exactly.

LOUIS: Someone who thinks of you at first dawn?

ANNIE: I don't know. Maybe.

LOUIS: Or right before sleep?

ANNIE: I don't think so.

Danger points continue to roll behind her.

LOUIS: And why do you think that is?

ANNIE: Sorry?

LOUIS: Why do you think no one cares for you in the special way people do?

ANNIE: 'Cause I'm a kid.

LOUIS: Not a kid. Princess. Prize. A reasonably attractive prize: it must be your personality.

ANNIE: My personality?

LOUIS: You must be lacking in a core component. Maybe you're no fun. Is that it?

ANNIE: I'm fun. I can be fun.

LOUIS: Prove it.

ANNIE: No, I don't think—

LOUIS: Show me how to reach the climax of this game.

ANNIE: I don't even know what that means!

LOUIS: There are lots of other princesses. Prettier. Smarter. Sweeter. Thinner. Taller. More attainable princesses who would share their achievements.

ANNIE: I can't. Don't want to. I have to go now.

He grabs her.

LOUIS: You're not being a team player.

ANNIE: So.

LOUIS: So your participation is necessary. Or it all falls down.

ANNIE: What falls down?

LOUIS: The game that we've been building for centuries.

ANNIE: Good! I want to build a new game.

LOUIS: There is nothing inadequate about the old game. The old game serves me.

ANNIE: But it doesn't serve me. It does me a disservice.

LOUIS: It works.

ANNIE: It's broken. Your game is broken.

LOUIS: It's been perfected.

50 | Megan Gail Coles

ANNIE: It's flawed and unfair.

LOUIS: It wasn't intended for you.

ANNIE: I'm going home.

LOUIS: You have no home.

ANNIE: Yes, I do.

LOUIS: A home requires other players.

ANNIE: There are other players at my home.

LOUIS: No. The people who should be there can't. And the rest have no time for princesses from icy kingdoms they've never been to and don't even wish to visit. It's only me. I'm the only one who cares, the only one who sees you on this path.

ANNIE's scoreboard reads "RUN."

ANNIE: That's not true.

LOUIS: It is and I see you for what you are. Scared. Tired. Alone. You're barely even here.

ANNIE: I'm here.

LOUIS: Not for long.

ANNIE's scoreboard reads " FASTER."

ANNIE: I have to go. I have to go now.

LOUIS: Fine. Go. Be gone, girl. Just like the rest.

ANNIE: Rest?

LOUIS: Where is that queen of yours? Or your king? Where's he? Why doesn't he escort you to your walled fortress?

ANNIE: The king? My father?

LOUIS: Fathers are for protecting daughters from people with unfriendly hearts.

ANNIE: My father doesn't live with us.

LOUIS: A kingdom without a king is always in danger of a mutiny.

ANNIE: That doesn't mean anything. You don't make any sense.

LOUIS: Every sad princess has a king who isn't waiting for her. Rule one.

ANNIE: He wasn't well.

LOUIS: You're no one's daughter. You're just a pile of parts.

ANNIE: Leave me alone.

LOUIS: I like your parts. They are satisfactory to me. I like your hair. Your eyes. Your arms. And your legs.

   LOUIS smells the inside of her arm.

You have nice parts.

LOUIS pulls her arm out straight.

I bet you're delicious.

ANNIE: I'm not delicious!

LOUIS: When I've had my fill of you, I'll wrap you in plastic and toss you in some wet place to be forgotten until you spoil and later make a bad smell.

ANNIE: No!

LOUIS licks her arm.

ANNIE's scoreboard blinks "RUN FASTER!"

Stop! No! Pause! Press pause!

Flashlight.

Then I think: no, no, here is how I die. One night I dance at the dance and boys see me. I don't wear jeans. I wear a skirt. Because I want to dance like a beautiful girl; I want them to see me, kind of, a little bit, and one does, a lot, and no one cares until later. Because little Native girls are disappearing forever like magic or mystery. Just vanished.

The flashlight goes out.

Poof.

Another flashlight turns off.

Gone.

ANNIE's flashlight goes out. Beat. Then it turns on again.

But not me. That's not the story I'm crafting here. This is a restart.

Real world. Food court. ANNIE approaches LOUIS's table.

LOUIS: What are you doing here?

ANNIE takes out an apple and wipes it on her shirt.

ANNIE: I'm learning from my mistakes and the mistakes of others.

LOUIS: What are you talking about? Where's Therese?

ANNIE: Therese is not coming.

LOUIS: But she said on the phone—

ANNIE: Therese told me what you did when she was making the beds.

LOUIS: What? I told you, she's a liar.

ANNIE: She told me you hurt other girls, too.

LOUIS: You told me she never said my name. Not once, you said.

ANNIE: Sometimes you can't name the ugly thing so you call it something else. Sometimes words get lost and people go looking for them in bottles. Then broomsticks go through the living-room ceiling; a fist goes through the pink kitchen wall. Boom. Smash. Grandmother Scotch-tapes blank sheets of printer paper over these gaps in judgment. There are eleven pieces of paper in her house. She writes the name on them. She's keeping a record of who went looking for their words on the other side of a hard surface: a wall, a window, a cheek.

LOUIS: Your grandmother can't help you. She's too old.

ANNIE: Anger lives in everyone regardless of their age, Louis. Which is just another list, really—the years you've been alive. This list is not the same length for everyone. It's shorter where I'm from. I've been taught not to expect as much. Because sometimes the candles on your very last birthday cake aren't very many, if you get a cake at all. So a birthday is not always something to be celebrated like a big deal. But this year is different. This year, I'm aging out. Therese told me what you did and I told Sharon.

LOUIS: What?

ANNIE: I told her and you're in big trouble now, mister.

LOUIS: Jesus.

ANNIE: You shouldn't swear, Louis. It's a weak form of communication.

LOUIS: It wasn't your secret to tell.

ANNIE: Everyone owns that kind of secret.

LOUIS: I never touched you.

ANNIE: Yet.

LOUIS: I wouldn't have.

ANNIE: Maybe not me. But someone. Another girl. A different girl.

LOUIS: Why would you do this to me?

ANNIE: Because you think a girl is just a kind of meat. Bits of flesh to tear from bones. Something to eat. Are you hungry, Louis? Are you hungry? I am. We all are. We're all starving animals searching for our next meal. Wolves, bunnies, wee birds in the tree. Taste, though, taste sets us apart. I have an old craving for heart from the inside of a freshly stalked seal. This ancient taste of mine is called brutal. They say: you're a brute, girl. And every time I want to scream: just because you didn't kill your food doesn't mean it didn't die! But I don't. Instead, I live on reservation. I'm reserved. Like something to return to when the urge is undeniable. You see, you think my body is on loan to me. That it's just a loaner body. Because I'm a girl and a girl is just something small for you to gnash. But you're wrong.

LOUIS: Are you for real?

ANNIE: Besides, it's what I wanted for my birthday. So I got it for myself. Sometimes you can't wait for someone else to get you what you want. You can't wish for it when you blow out the candles and hope it comes true. Sometimes hope is not nearly as active as a person needs to be. Especially when it's this important. When it's this important a person needs action; when it's this important you have to get it for yourself.

She bites into the apple.

I decided I'm going to eat apples all the time now. I'm only putting good things inside. I'm going to fill myself up with things that make me strong and brave like an adult. Not weak and scared like a little kid. Canada says I'm grown up now so I'm going to start thinking about grown-up things. Not all the time because that's boring. But sometimes because it's necessary. Sharon said it was a very grown-up call I made. She's really proud of me. I'm really proud of me, too.

She's really angry with you though. And I'm really angry with you, too, Louis.

LOUIS: Oh my god, I have to get out of here. I can't believe you would do this, you dirty little sq—

ANNIE: Don't say it. Don't even think it.

LOUIS: After everything I did for you—

ANNIE: You did nothing for me, at least, nothing good. You did nothing good for me.

LOUIS: I bought you fries.

ANNIE: And you kept the change. Every time. I know how numbers work—I count, I keep track every day in the games I play.

LOUIS: You're awful.

ANNIE: You're awful. And you're out of lives. No more girls for you.

LOUIS: None.

ANNIE throws her apple core in the trash.

Annie—

LOUIS grabs ANNIE by the wrist. She looks up in his face.

You can't decide when my mission is terminated.

ANNIE: I can. I already did. I'm not afraid of you anymore. Or men like you. So you have no power left. We're done here. Game over.

LOUIS lets go. He has been beaten. The scoreboard reads level three is complete. He looks around desperately and leaves. ANNIE stands there alone. To herself:

I win.

ISAAC arrives.

ISAAC: What'd you win?

ANNIE: Oh, hey!

ISAAC: What'd you win?

ANNIE: Just this round.

ISAAC: Cool. I guess.

Beat.

So my mom said you can stay at our house for a while.

ANNIE: Really?

ISAAC: Yeah, I mean, it took some doing but she said yeah. She says there's going to be a tidal wave of paperwork.

ANNIE: Aren't all waves tidal waves?

ISAAC: Yeah, moms are ridiculous.

ANNIE: That was nice of her though. Please tell her thank you but I can't.

ISAAC: What do you mean you can't?

ANNIE: I'm not staying here.

ISAAC: Where are you going?

ANNIE: Home to visit Grandmother.

ISAAC: Are you serious? I've been fighting with my mom about this for weeks.

ANNIE: I didn't ask you to do that.

ISAAC: I did it for you.

ANNIE: Not my responsibility.

ISAAC: You're not even grateful.

ANNIE: I'm— Thanks, but no thanks.

ISAAC: Girls. Sheesh.

ANNIE: Sheesh.

ISAAC: Hey, you're not the parrot. I'm the parrot!

ANNIE: You're the parrot?

ISAAC: Yeah.

ANNIE: Okay. I want you to kiss me.

ISAAC: What?

ANNIE: I want you to kiss me.

ISAAC: Um, I want you to kiss me?

ANNIE kisses ISAAC. The game world celebrates in you-win style until they stop.

ANNIE: How was that?

ISAAC: Um, my, yeah, better than a pickle.

ANNIE: Great. Happy birthday to me!

ISAAC: Today's your birthday?

ANNIE: Yup. I'm all aged out. No longer a ward of the state.

ISAAC: That's great. Right? That's good, right?

ANNIE: It can be. I hope so.

ISAAC: Awesome. Awesome. We should celebrate. We should do something . . . together.

ANNIE: Like what?

ISAAC: Whatever you want, it's your birthday!

ANNIE: Okay. All right.

ISAAC: So what do you want to do?

ANNIE: Go outside. I want to be outside, Isaac. Can we go to a park? I would like to walk in the forest.

ISAAC: I know the perfect place!

ANNIE: Great.

They begin to leave.

I actually hate the mall.

ISAAC: Me too.

ANNIE: Then why do you hang out here?

ISAAC: I thought you might be here.

He reaches for her hand.

ANNIE: Sheesh, you really are adorkable.

The End

Glossary

This glossary uses material from Wiktionary, released under the Creative Commons Attribution-Share-Alike License 3.0 (https://creativecommons.org/licenses/by-sa/3.0/).

ACCOUNTABILITY: 1. The state of being accountable. **2.** Liability to be called on to render an account. **3.** Accountableness, responsible for, answerable for.

AGENCY: The capacity, condition or state of acting or of exerting power.

COLONIALISM: 1. The colonial domination policy. **2.** A colonial system.

CONSENT: To express willingness, to give permission.

COURAGE: The ability to do things which one finds frightening.

EQUALITY: The state of being equal, especially in status, rights and opportunities.

EXPLOITATION: The act or result of forcibly depriving someone of something to which they have a natural right.

FEMINISM: **1.** The theory of the political, economic and social equality of the sexes. **2.** Organized activity on behalf of women's rights and interests.

HUMAN RIGHTS: The basic rights and freedoms that all humans should be guaranteed, such as the right to life and liberty, freedom of thought and expression and equality before the law.

INDIGENOUS: **1.** Born or engendered in, native to a land or region, especially before an intrusion. **2.** Of or relating to the native inhabitants of a land.

INTERSECTIONAL: Of or pertaining to an intersection, especially of multiple forms of discrimination.

MARGINALIZE: **1.** To relegate something (especially a topic or a group of people) to the margins or to a lower limit. **2.** To exclude socially.

MISOGYNY: Hatred of, contempt for or prejudice against women.

OPPRESSION: **1.** The exercise of authority or power in a burdensome, cruel or unjust manner. **2.** The act of oppressing, or the state of being oppressed. **3.** A feeling of being oppressed.

PATRIARCHY: **1.** A social system in which the father is head of the household, having authority over women and children, and in which lineage is traced through the male line. **2.** A power structure in which men are dominant.

RACISM: **1.** The belief that one race or ethnic group is superior or inferior to another race or group of races. **2.** Prejudice or discrimination based upon race or ethnicity. **3.** A hierarchical system that benefits one race at the expense of all others.

RESERVATION: A tract of land set apart for the use of an Indigenous group.

RESILIENCE: The mental ability to recover quickly from depression, illness or misfortune.

REVOLUTION: A sudden, vast change in a situation, a discipline or the way of thinking and behaving.

SEXISM: 1. The belief that people of one sex or gender are inherently superior to people of the other sex or gender. **2.** Different treatment or discrimination based on a difference of sex or gender. **3.** Disadvantage or unequal opportunity arising from the cultural dominance of one gender over the other. **3.** Promotion or expectation or assumption of people to behave in accordance with or deviate from a gender role.

Acknowledgements

I would like to extend my sincere gratitude to Annie Gibson, Blake Sproule and Jessica Lewis at Playwrights Canada Press as well as the exceptional teams at Geordie Productions, Playwrights' Workshop Montréal and the Playwrights Guild of Canada.

All my love and loyalty to my friends for their support and kindness, especially to Maria, Andreae and Elisabeth. Also, much gratitude to Robert Chafe for his constant encouragement, ready ear and thoughtful advice. And, of course, to Emma Tibaldo for being an inspiration and constant source of strength over the last decade.

A special thank you to my big Newfoundland family: aunts, uncles and cousins. To my sisters, Melissa, Chelsie and Alicia. To my mom and dad, Della and Nelson Coles.

Also, to my pop, Stephen Dredge, a gentleman who always listens when women speak and sets the nice man standard ever higher with his considerate and generous manner of being present in our lives.

Most of all, thank you to my nan, Susan, who gifted me all the bones that make up my face, this wicked sense of humour, a great appreciation of nature and the need to question everything including autocracy and complacency. I love you so much every day without skipping a beat forever until there is nary a tree left in our whole forest.

And I think your hands are beautiful.

Megan Gail Coles is a graduate of Memorial University and the National Theatre School of Canada, and is currently completing the UBC M.F.A. Opt-Res program. She is Co-Founder and Artistic Director of Poverty Cove Theatre Company. She is presently working on her debut novel (House of Anansi, 2017) and the Driftwood Trilogy of plays. Megan's first fiction collection, *Eating Habits of the Chronically Lonesome* (Killick), won the BMO Winterset Award, the ReLit Award and the Margaret & John Savage First Book Award, and earned her the one-time Writers' Trust Five x Five prize. Originally from Savage Cove on the Great Northern Peninsula, Megan now resides in St. John's, where she is also Executive Director of *Riddle Fence*.

First edition: November 2017
Printed and bound in Canada by Rapido Books, Montreal

Cover art, *Les grands vents*, by Dominique Fortin, www.lafeedargent.com
Author photo © David Howells, www.davidhowellsphoto.com

PLAYWRIGHTS CANADA PRESS

202-269 Richmond St. W.
Toronto, ON
M5V 1X1

416.703.0013
info@playwrightscanada.com
www.playwrightscanada.com
@playcanpress